# Ballet
# Party™

by M. J. Carr

DUALSTAR PUBLICATIONS  PARACHUTE PRESS

SCHOLASTIC INC.
New York   Toronto   London   Auckland   Sydney

DUALSTAR PUBLICATIONS  PARACHUTE PRESS

Dualstar Publications
c/o 10100 Santa Monica Blvd.
Suite 2200
Los Angeles, CA 90067

Parachute Press, Inc.
156 Fifth Avenue
Suite 325
New York, NY 10010

Published by Scholastic Inc.

With special thanks to Robert Thorne and Harold Weitzberg.

Printed in the U.S.A.
November 1998
ISBN: 0-590-29399-0
A B C D E F G H I J

"Don't you love going to the ballet?" Ashley asked me as she stuffed her jeans into our suitcase. "I just love to watch the ballerinas leap and twirl on the stage."

"But the very best part is seeing all the beautiful, fancy costumes," I said.

"No way!" Ashley said. "The dancing is the best part."

I'm Mary-Kate Olsen. My twin sister, Ashley, and I are nine years old. We both have strawberry blond hair and big, blue eyes. We look alike, but we don't always think alike.

There is one thing we *always* agree on, though. We love to have parties. And our next one was sure to be the best party ever!

"I'm so excited," Ashley said. "This is going to be the *ultimate* ballet party."

"We'll fly to New York City," I said. "And meet our friends Stephanie and Dana who live there."

"Then we'll all take a ballet class with the New York City Ballet," Ashley added. "And finally, we'll watch the ballet perform at the famous Lincoln Center!"

"I can't wait until the curtain rises," I said.

"Me neither," Ashley agreed. "I hope we have good seats!"

"Seats?" I said. "We won't be sitting. We'll be on the stage—dancing in beautiful costumes!" I grabbed my pink tutu and whirled around the room, imagining being on stage. "It'll be like a dream come true."

"That's a dream, all right," Ashley said with a laugh. "A *day* dream. Believe me, Mary-Kate. It takes years and years to become a ballerina."

"Maybe for you," I replied. "But you just wait—*I'm* going to be up there dancing in the spotlight."

After all, how hard could it be to become a ballerina?

Ashley made a list of things to pack while I collected our clothes.

"We'll need clothes for ballet class," she reminded me. "That means leotards—"

"Check," I replied.

"Tights," she added.

"Check."

"Legwarmers. Ballet slippers."

"Check. Check," I said.

"And don't forget our party dresses for opening night at the ballet," Ashley said. "I think that's all we need."

I stuffed all our clothes into the suitcase and pressed down on the lid. "I can't wait to go!" I told my sister. "There's just one problem,"

"Oh," Ashley said. "So you've finally realized that you won't be able to dance on stage?"

"Nope," I said. "The problem is that our suitcase won't shut!"

New York City was bigger and busier than I imagined. I couldn't wait to go exploring.

I peered out the window of our hotel room. Outside stood a beautiful horse and a shiny wooden carriage.

"Hey!" I cried, pointing to the horse and carriage. "Let's take a ride!"

"That does look like fun," Ashley said. "But we need to get ready for our ballet lesson. Stephanie and Dana will be waiting for us."

"Please," I begged. "Just a quick ride? We've come all the way to New York City. We have to see the sights!"

Ashley thought a moment. "Okay," she agreed finally. "We have a little time to spare. Let's go!"

We clip-clopped all over the city. We saw Times Square and all the famous theaters on Broadway. We saw the Empire State Building, the Statue of Liberty, and—our favorite—the Twin Towers.

We were having so much fun, we totally lost track of time.

"Oh, no!" Ashley cried when she looked at her watch. "We're going to be late for our lesson!"

She leaned forward in her seat. "Lincoln Center, please," she called to our carriage driver. "And step on it!"

The carriage dropped us off in front of Lincoln Center—the place where the New York City Ballet performs.

"Come on," Ashley cried. "We have to meet someone from the ballet in the theater." She pointed to a building with huge windows.

Inside, the theater was enormous. We looked out over a sea of red velvet seats. The ceiling above us looked like a night sky, full of bright stars.

"Wow!" Ashley gasped. "Imagine being a ballerina and dancing on this big stage."

Soon, we won't have to *imagine* it, I thought. We'll be *doing* it.

I was so busy gazing around the theater that I didn't notice someone had joined us.

"Excuse me," a voice said. "You must be Mary-Kate and Ashley." The voice belonged to a beautiful ballerina. Her shiny brown hair was knotted on top of her head. She wore a sleek black leotard. "My name is Danielle."

"Nice to meet you," Ashley said. "Sorry we're late."

"We wouldn't miss this for the world!" I cried.

Danielle smiled. "Follow me, girls. Your friends are already changed and ready for our class."

Stephanie and Dana were waiting for us in the ballet studio. We rushed over to say hi.

"I can't believe we're here at the New York City Ballet!" Dana squealed.

"This is going to be the greatest party ever!" Stephanie exclaimed.

"Welcome to ballet class, everyone," Danielle said. "Come over here next to the barre, please." We all hurried over.

"We have a lot to learn today," she told us. "First I'd like to show you *port de bras*. Does anyone know what that means?"

Ashley piped up. "Isn't that the different positions for your arms?" she asked.

"Very good, Ashley," Danielle said. Then she began to move her arms gracefully—up, down and around. I tried to follow along, but it was really hard to get it right. I glanced at Ashley. She seemed to know just what to do.

"I think you have a knack for this," I whispered to her.

"That's because I've taken a *lot* of ballet classes," she replied.

Hmmm. I guess I had some catching up to do. No problem, I thought. I'll be moving my arms like that in no time.

Next, Danielle showed us the different positions for the feet. And then she taught us how to do *pliés*. "Bend your knees," she told us.

"Now let's try some *tendus*," Danielle said. She showed us how to lift one leg straight out in front. "Point your toes," she instructed.

My legs were getting tired. Becoming a ballerina was hard work!

I stepped away from the barre to take a break.

"Where are you going, Mary-Kate?" Danielle asked.

"My ballet slippers are a little too tight," I lied. I couldn't admit that I was tired already.

"Okay, when you've fixed them, come back to the barre and we'll try *arabesque*."

Arabesque? What was that? I wondered.

We all gathered around as Danielle demonstrated *arabesque*. She lifted her leg behind her and pointed it straight to the ceiling.

"Wow!" I cried. "That's incredible! I *have* to learn how to do that!"

"Okay, now you try it," Danielle said.

Ashley and Stephanie and Dana had no trouble balancing on one leg. But me? I almost fell flat on my face. Good thing I had the barre to hold on to.

"And now," Danielle said, "I want everyone in the center of the room. We'll do some steps away from the barre."

With nothing to hold onto? Uh-oh!

Danielle showed us how to do *pirouettes*. We spun around and around.

Whoa! Ballet practice was making me dizzy! But I loved it!

Just keep working at it, Mary-Kate, I told myself. If you're going to dance with the New York City Ballet, you have to...

...practice,
practice,
practice!

Danielle clapped her hands together. "Okay, everyone. Great job! Now I have to go to rehearsal."

"Didn't you just rehearse?" I asked.

"That was class," Danielle explained. "Now I have to practice my routine for the ballet. It's opening night tonight."

"Can we watch you rehearse?" Ashley asked.

"Of course," Danielle replied.

Wow! A real rehearsal. With real ballerinas! On opening night!

Our party was getting better and better!

Two dancers were waiting for Danielle at rehearsal. Danielle switched on the music.

The male dancer leaped straight up in the air. He jumped so high, it looked as if he were bouncing on a trampoline!

Danielle rehearsed her part. She twirled, she leaped, she glided across the stage! The steps she danced were much harder than the ones we had learned in class!

All the dancers danced so gracefully. They made everything look so easy!

"Would you like to try some of these steps?" Danielle asked when the other dancers took a break.

"Yes!" Ashley, Stephanie, Dana and I all cried together.

"Let the music inspire you," Danielle coached us as we lined up on stage. "Really listen to the music. It will help you."

I concentrated hard on the music. I tried swooping when the music swooped, and spinning when the music spun. Danielle was right. That made it a lot easier. And it was fun, too.

Maybe I could learn some of the steps in time for opening night. Just maybe....

"I'm starving!" Stephanie suddenly cried. "Do dancers just rehearse all day?"

Danielle laughed. "Okay," she said. "Why don't we take a break. There's a cafeteria downstairs. We'll grab a bite to eat."

"Yay!" we cheered.

Stephanie and Dana ran down the stairs. I hobbled after them.

"What's wrong with your feet?" Ashley asked me.

I took off one of my ballet slippers. "Whoa!" I said, staring down at my feet. "I have a blister the size of California on my big toe."

Ashley giggled.

"Is something the matter?" Danielle asked.

"There's a blister on my sister!" Ashley announced.

"Put your feet up at lunch," Danielle suggested. "Your toes deserve a rest. They worked hard today."

Lots of dancers had gathered for lunch in the cafeteria. They were all tall and graceful and beautiful. They didn't seem to have sore feet like I did.

Suddenly it hit me. Could Ashley be right? Was our dancing on stage just a silly dream?

I watched in amazement as the other dancers ate lunch, then leaped to their feet and pranced across the room. Didn't they ever get tired?

I massaged my feet under the table. Ballet was hard. Much harder than I had expected.

I was never going to dance as gracefully as Danielle and the other dancers, I realized. It was going to take more than practice. It would take some kind of magic.

I closed my eyes and wished as hard as I could. If only I could dance like Danielle. Just for one night....

"A penny for your thoughts," Danielle said.

"Oh, w-well" I stammered. "I was just thinking about how beautiful ballet is."

"Do you want to see something really beautiful?" she asked. "Come with me to the costume shop. I have to go for the final fitting of my costume for tonight."

"Yay!" we all cried.

Maybe I'll find a costume for myself, I thought. Just in case my wish comes true....

The costume shop was filled with colorful tutus, sparkly costumes, satin toe shoes, hats, ribbons, and everything a ballerina needs.

Dana ran her hand across a white tutu. "Ooh," she said. "It's so beautiful!"

Ashley grabbed two black hats. She clapped one on top of my head. "Let's dance," she said.

She pulled me up onto a table, and we started dancing. I felt like I was on stage. It was great fun!

Stephanie and Dana cheered.

Just then, Danielle stepped out of the dressing room. She was wearing her costume. It was pale pink with glittery trim. She looked so elegant.

"I have a great idea," Danielle said. "When I'm done here, let's head to Central Park. It's just a short walk away. It's a very magical place." Danielle winked at me.

Magical, huh? A visit to Central Park sounded like just what I needed to make my wish come true.

Central Park was green and quiet and peaceful. It was hard to believe we were in the middle of busy New York City.

As we strolled through the park, Danielle told the story of her favorite ballet, *Swan Lake*. We crossed a bridge and stopped at a calm, glassy lake in the park.

"How do you dance like a swan?" I asked.

"Imagine you're a beautiful bird," she replied, "with a long, graceful neck and gorgeous white wings." Danielle fluttered her arms as if they were wings. I glanced at her reflection in the lake.

"Look!" I cried. I pointed at her reflection. It looked like a real swan!

Hmmm. Maybe there really was something magical about Central Park. If the magic in the park could work for Danielle, maybe it could work for me, too.

I snuck behind a tree and called to Ashley and my friends to join me. "Come on!" I cried.

I closed my eyes and wished really hard for the four of us to change into beautiful swans.

Suddenly...it happened! We all looked like swans! With fluffy white tutus and feathery caps!

"Surprise!" we cried as we ran back out.

Danielle gasped.

Around and around the park we danced. Around the lake. Across a meadow. Around park benches.

Was it real? Or was I dreaming?

Danielle showed us how to dance the steps to *Swan Lake*. And the people strolling by made the perfect audience.

Soon the sky turned pink as the sun began to set.

"Oh, no!" Danielle cried as she glanced at her watch. "It's late! I have to get back to the theater or I'll miss opening night!"

We raced back to Lincoln Center as fast as we could. Danielle rushed to get ready. She sat at her dressing table. Her hands shook as she picked up a black pencil. She drew a dark line across her eyelid.

"You don't need so much makeup," I told Danielle. "You're already beautiful."

"Yes," Stephanie agreed.

"Thanks, girls. But I have to put the makeup on really thick when I go on stage," she said. "Otherwise, the audience won't be able to see my face in all the bright lights."

Suddenly, Danielle knocked a small bottle off the table. Makeup spilled everywhere.

"Oh, no!" she cried. "I guess I have first-night jitters."

"But why would *you* be nervous?" Dana asked. "You've danced on stage lots of times before."

"I'm always nervous before I go on stage," Danielle replied. "Especially on opening night."

I thought a moment. "Danielle, I think I know what the problem is," I said. "Open your mouth."

Danielle opened her mouth, and I peered down her throat. I nodded to Ashley. "Just as I thought."

Ashley looked too. "Hmmm. A severe case of butterflies in the stomach!"

Danielle laughed.

"But don't worry," I said. "We know what to do."

"Take a deep breath," Ashley told Danielle.

"And don't forget to smile," I reminded her. "Just go out there and have fun."

Danielle sighed. "That's good advice," she said. "But I'm afraid I still have butterflies in my stomach."

"It could be worse," I said. "You could have a caterpillar up your nose!"

Danielle giggled. Suddenly, she didn't look *quite* so nervous.

"Would you girls like to watch me from backstage?" Danielle asked. "You can stand in the wings. That's the area right next to the stage. You'll be able to see everything from there."

"We'd love to!" I cried. Then I glanced down at our clothes. Uh-oh. We were still wearing our leotards. We had to change into our party dresses. And fast!

"Come on!" I said to Ashley. "Let's get dressed!"

"But, Mary-Kate," Ashley cried, "our hotel is a long way away. We'll never make it back in time!"

"We'll make it if we hurry!" I told Ashley.

We raced back to our hotel and quickly changed into our party dresses. When we returned, Danielle was ready to go on stage.

The door of the dressing room swung open.

"One minute until curtain!" the stage manager called.

"Wish me luck!" Danielle smiled as she left the room.

Dana, Stephanie, Ashley and I all hurried into the wings.

I peered out at the audience. Every seat in every balcony was filled! No wonder Danielle had the jitters!

Danielle danced beautifully. When her partner lifted her, it looked almost as if she were flying.

As I watched, I imagined it was me out there, dressed like a princess in a long, white tutu. I was being lifted effortlessly onto the shoulder of a handsome prince. Mary-Kate Olsen, the greatest ballerina of them all….

Suddenly, I was awakened from my daydream. The audience was applauding loudly. Danielle stepped in front of the curtain to take her bows.

"We're going to go meet our parents," Stephanie said. She and Dana waved goodbye.

A woman appeared beside us in the wings. She held two beautiful bouquets of flowers. "Would you girls like to give these to Danielle?" she asked.

"You mean, go out there? In front of all those people?" Ashley replied.

"Exactly," the woman said. "Would you like to?"

"Yes!" Ashley and I cried together.

We each carried a big bouquet of colorful flowers to the center of the stage. We carefully laid them across Danielle's arms. Danielle beamed at us.

Ashley nudged me. "I guess you were right," she said. "We got to go on stage after all!"

"Hey, look!" I cried. "It's Dana and Stephanie." Our friends waved wildly at us from the audience. They looked surprised to see us up there.

I felt really great up on stage in front of all those people.

But I still wished that I could be up there dancing for the audience.

"You were wonderful," I told Danielle when she returned to her dressing room.

"Thank you," she replied with a big smile. "Every time I step onto the stage, I forget all my fears. All I remember is that I love to dance."

Ashley looked at her watch. It was getting late. Our party was just about over. We had already said goodbye to our friends.

"Danielle, thanks for everything today," Ashley said. "You taught us so much."

"Yes," I added. "I learned that it takes a lot of work to be a ballerina. I guess I won't be dancing out on that big stage any time soon."

"Sure you will," Danielle replied with a wink. "Maybe sooner than you think."

"But how?" I asked.

"Didn't you come to New York to have the *ultimate* ballet party?" she said with a mysterious smile.

"Yes, but—" I started.

"Come with me," she said.

In a twinkling, Ashley and I were standing with Danielle on the stage of the New York City Ballet.

Beyond the footlights, I could see the audience. They were staring straight at us!

Ashley was wearing a beautiful pink tutu. And so was I! On our heads were crowns of pink roses.

In my beautiful costume, I felt elegant and graceful. Just like Danielle.

In the orchestra pit, the conductor raised his baton. The music began. And then, as if by magic, we whirled across the stage. We danced like prima ballerinas, our toes perfectly pointed, our pirouettes crisp and clean.

When the music ended, the audience burst into applause.

As we took our bows, I grinned at Ashley. She nudged me. "I can't believe it!" she whispered.

We looked up into the balconies. People clapped and cheered.

"This really did turn out to be the ultimate ballet party, didn't it," Ashley said.

"Like a dream come true," I agreed.

Hi from the both of us,

    Thanks for coming to our Ballet
Party!
    We hope you like the special ballet
hair band we have for you.
    And we can't wait to see you at
our next fun party!

Love,

Ashley + Mary-Kate
Olsen     Olsen